rge

shrinks

by
WILLIAM JOYCE

ATHENEUM
BOOKS FOR YOUNG READERS
New York   London   Toronto   Sydney   New Delhi

One day, while his mother and father were out, George dreamed he was small, and when he woke up, he found it was true.

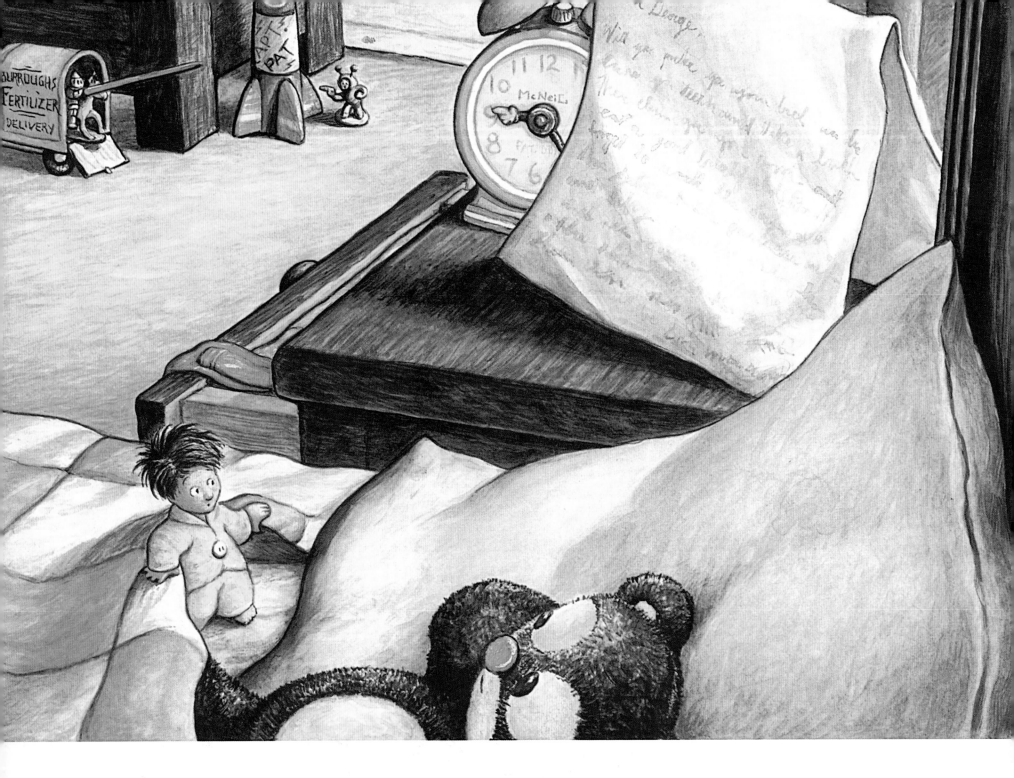

His parents had left him a note. It read:

"Dear George, when you wake up,

please make your bed,

brush your teeth,

and take a bath.

Then clean up your room

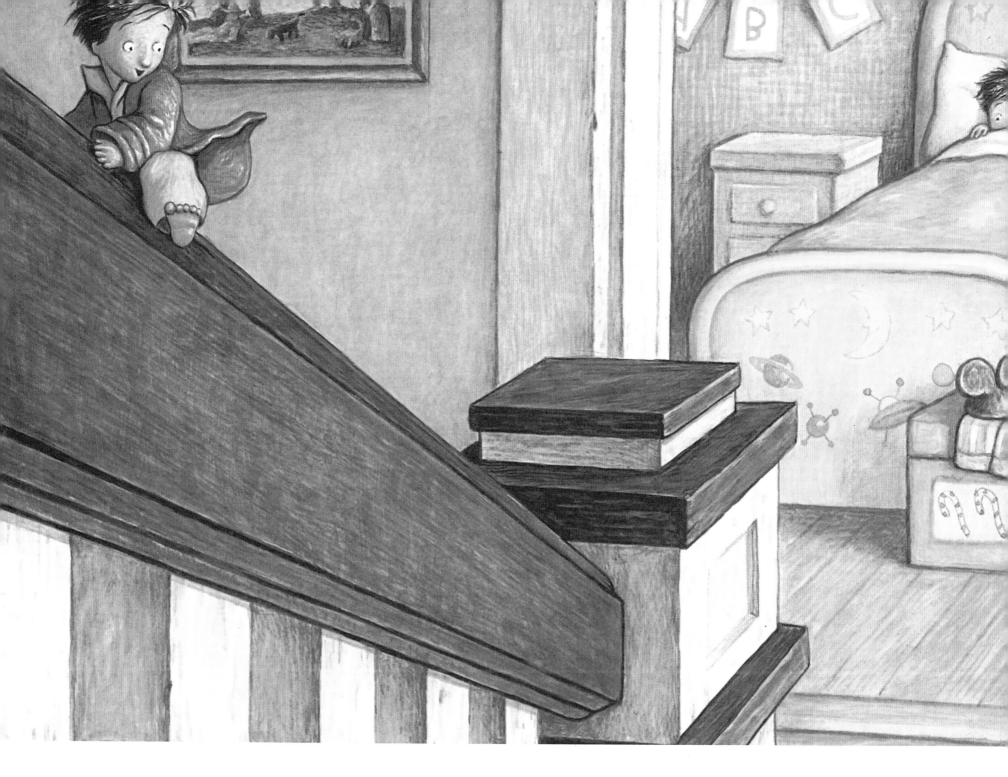

and go get your little brother.

Eat a good breakfast,

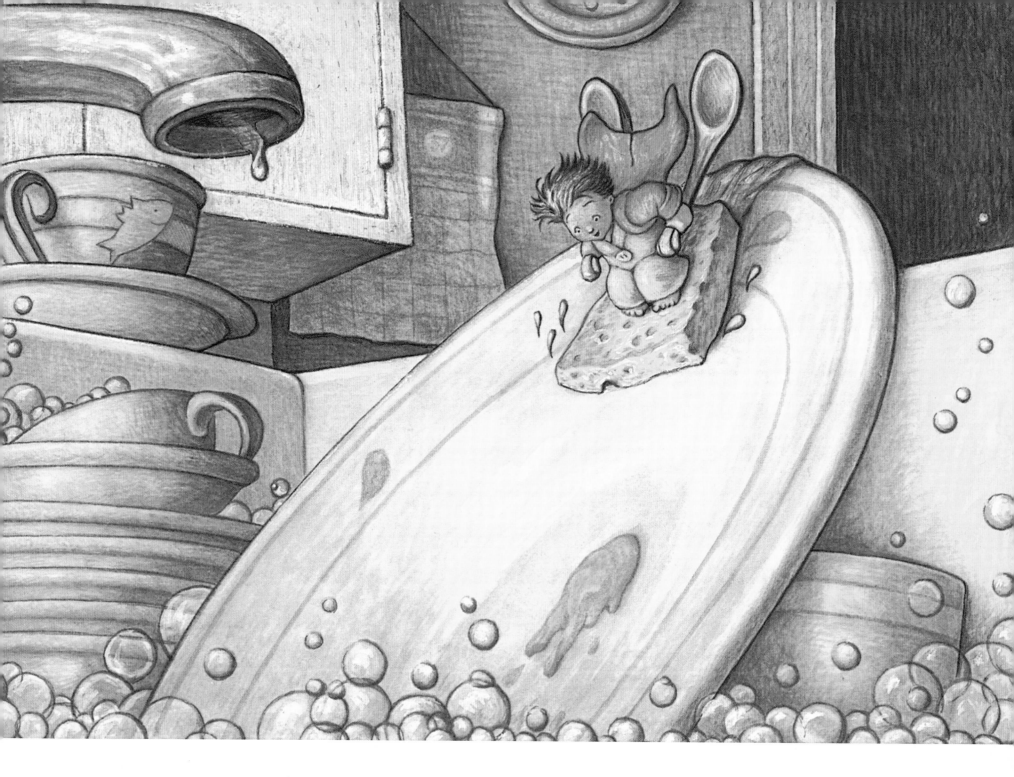

and don't forget to wash the dishes, dear.

Do your homework.

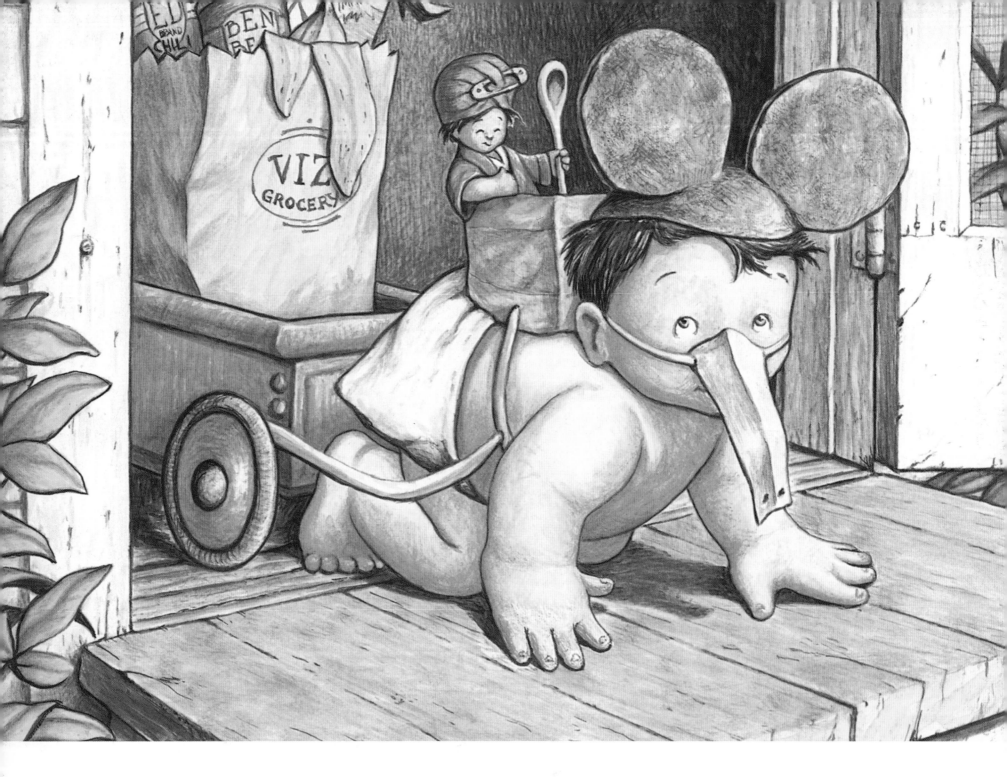

Take out the garbage,

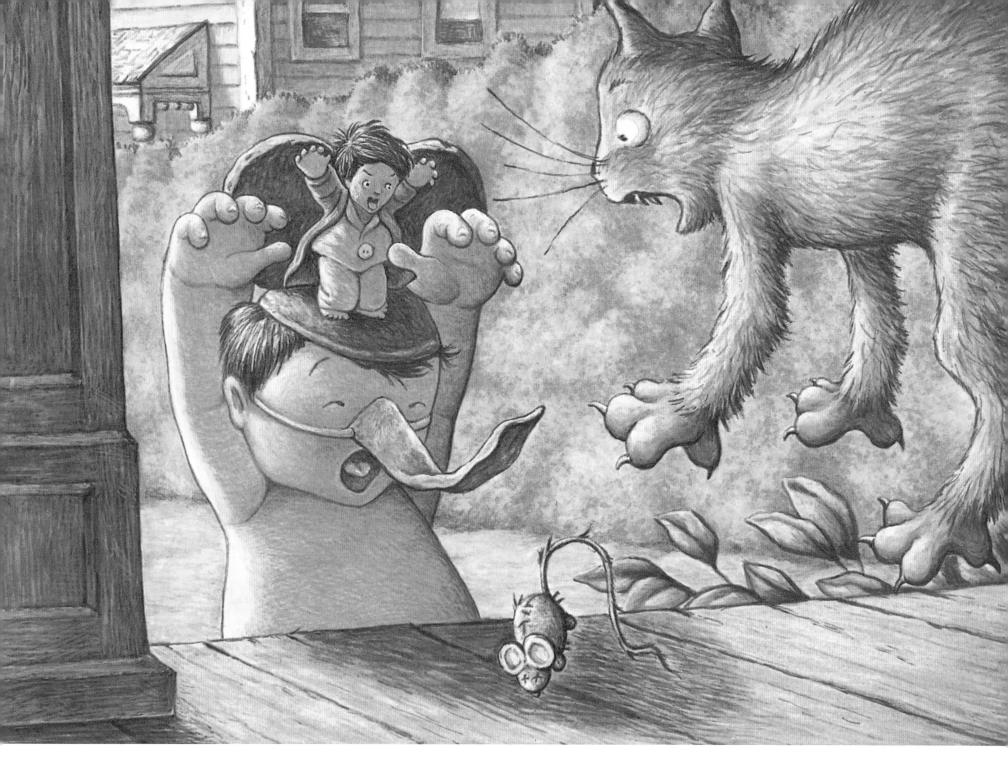

and play quietly.

Make sure you water the plants

and feed the fish.

Then check the mail

and get some fresh air.

Try to stay out of trouble,

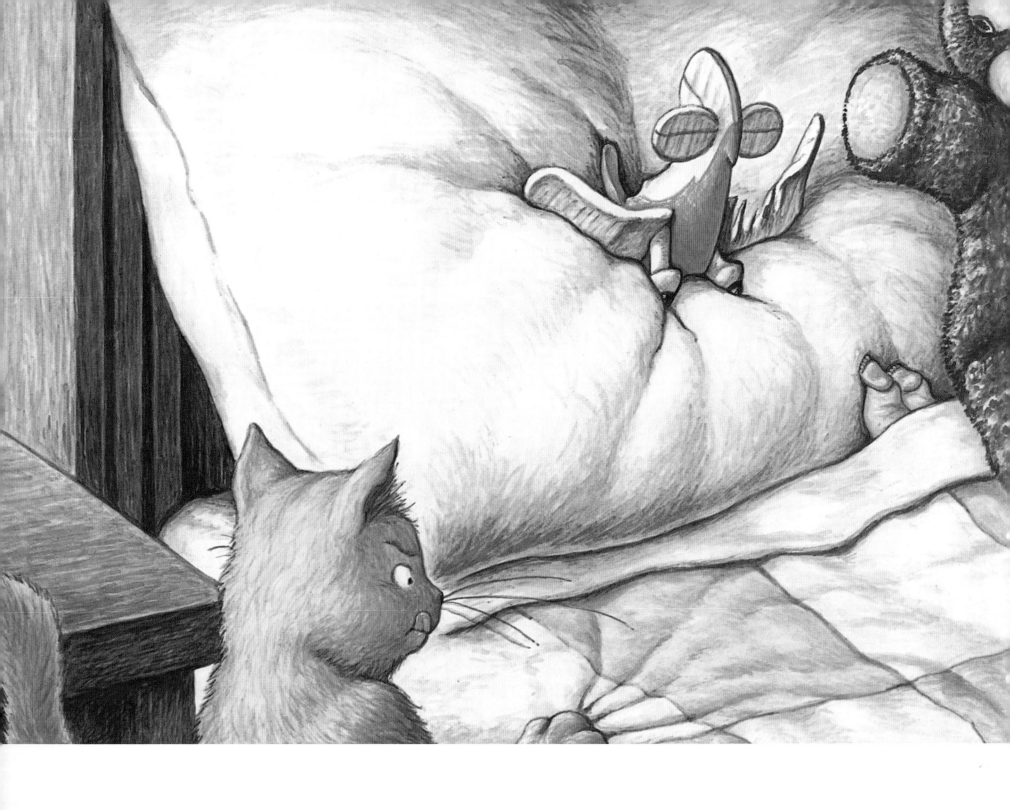

and we'll be home soon.

Love, Mom and Dad."

for NATE

A
atheneum

ATHENEUM BOOKS FOR YOUNG READERS
An imprint of Simon & Schuster Children's Publishing Division
1230 Avenue of the Americas, New York, New York 10020
Text and interior illustrations copyright © 1985 by William Joyce
Jacket illustrations copyright © 1985, 2000 by William Joyce
Originally published in 1985 by Laura Geringer Books/HarperCollins Publishers.
All rights reserved, including the right of reproduction in whole or in part in any form.
ATHENEUM BOOKS FOR YOUNG READERS is a registered trademark of Simon & Schuster, Inc.
Atheneum logo is a trademark of Simon & Schuster, Inc.
For information about special discounts for bulk purchases, please contact
Simon & Schuster Special Sales at 1-866-506-1949 or business@simonandschuster.com.
The Simon & Schuster Speakers Bureau can bring authors to your live event.
For more information or to book an event, contact the Simon & Schuster Speakers Bureau at
1-866-248-3049 or visit our website at www.simonspeakers.com.
Book design by Alicia Mikles
The text for this book was set in Engine and Providence Sans.
The illustrations for this book were rendered in watercolor.
Manufactured in China • 0417 SCP
First Atheneum Books for Young Readers Edition
2 4 6 8 10 9 7 5 3 1
CIP data for this book is available from the Library of Congress.
ISBN 978-1-4814-8953-9
ISBN 978-1-4814-8954-6 (eBook)